THE
Christmas Snowman

A STORY BY *Margery Cuyler*

ILLUSTRATED BY

Johanna Westerman

Sky Pony Press • New York

For my dearest cousin Mary,
with thanks for providing the atmosphere
in which this story could take place —M. C.

For John —J. W.

Text copyright © 1992, 2011 by Margery Cuyler
Illustrations copyright © 1992, 2011 by Johanna Westerman

Sky Pony Press books may be purchased in bulk at special discounts for sales promotion, corporate gifts, fund-raising, or educational purposes. Special editions can also be created to specifications. For details, contact the Special Sales Department, Sky Pony Press, 307 West 36th Street, 11th Floor, New York, NY 10018 or info@skyhorsepublishing.com.

Sky Pony® is a registered trademark of Skyhorse Publishing, Inc.®, a Delaware corporation.

Visit our website at www.skyhorsepublishing.com.

Manufactured in China, May 2011
This product conforms to CPSIA 2008

10 9 8 7 6 5 4 3 2 1

Library of Congress Cataloging-in-Publication Data is available on file.
ISBN: 978-1-61608-483-7

THE CHRISTMAS SNOWMAN

It was only two weeks until Christmas. Mama was busy baking cookies. Papa was busy making a stand for the fir tree he had chopped down near the pond.

Kevin and Sally were busy wrapping presents. But they were tired of being inside. It had been snowing for three days, and now the sun was out.

"Let's make a snowman," said Sally.

"A big one," said Kevin. "Big like Santa."

Sally and Kevin bundled up in their warmest clothes and ran to the field next to the barn.

First Sally made the bottom. She rolled a snowball around the field until it was as big as a boulder. Then Kevin made the middle. He rolled his snowball until it was the size of a huge pumpkin. Next they rolled a ball for the head. It was the size of a soccer ball.

"Now he needs a face," said Kevin.

They fetched two pieces of charcoal for his eyes, a carrot for his nose, and radishes for his mouth. They patted and shaped more snow into arms and legs. They dressed him in mittens, one of Papa's old vests, and a raccoon hat they found in the barn. Then Sally took off her scarf and wrapped it around his neck.

"What should we name our snowman?" asked Kevin.

"Let's call him Mr. Snow," said Sally.

For the next few days, Mr. Snow stood cold and white in the middle of the field while Sally and Kevin played.

They lay on their backs and made angels as they looked up at the lacy pine branches above.

They built snow forts as high as the window in the maple sugar shed.

They went sledding on Bucket Hill, falling into a heap after flying across the bridge.

They crisscrossed the field on their skis, making circles and squares.

One day they went skating with Mama and Papa on the pond. The blades of their skates clicked in the cold afternoon air as they zigzagged across the ice.

And always, Mr. Snow stood like a friendly statue as everyone played nearby.

A week before Christmas, the moon was full. As the moonlight fell on Sally's face, she woke up. She ran over to the window and looked out. Could it be? Mr. Snow was glowing like the angel on top of the Christmas tree. And he was moving his arms up and down stiffly, like a puppet.

Sally ran into Kevin's room.

"Wake up!" she cried. "Wake up!"

"What's wrong?" asked Kevin.

"It's Mr. Snow," said Sally. "Come and see!"

Together they knelt at Kevin's window and gazed out at the white world beyond.

Now Mr. Snow was lying down. Sliding his arms and legs back and forth through the snow, he was making an angel. His mouth was turned up at the corners in a broad radish smile.

Sally gasped as Mr. Snow got to his knees. He began packing snow into blocks to make a snow fort. The walls grew so high that soon Sally could only see his raccoon hat over the top.

Then Mr. Snow punched out a door and stepped through. Next he walked to the barn and disappeared inside.

"Do you think he'll come back?" asked Sally.

"I don't know," whispered Kevin.

But he did. He reappeared carrying the sled. He climbed to the top of Bucket Hill. Then he flopped down on his belly and flew down the slope and across the bridge.

After sledding on the hill a few times, Mr. Snow walked back to the barn. This time he came out carrying Papa's skis, poles, boots, and skates.

First he went to the pond. He whirled around the ice, the blades of his skates shimmering in the moonlight.

"Do you think he's whistling?" asked Kevin.

"Maybe," said Sally. "Or maybe he's just humming Christmas carols to himself."

Finally, Mr. Snow put on Papa's boots and skis. Like a pale shadow, he glided across the field.

"Are we dreaming?" asked Kevin.

"No," said Sally. "I always knew Mr. Snow was special."

"Still, we'd better go to sleep," said Kevin. "Mr. Snow wouldn't like it if he knew we were watching."

Sally yawned.

"I guess you're right," she said as she walked back to her room.

In the morning, Kevin and Sally ran outdoors to see Mr. Snow. He was as cold and white as the day they had made him. His snow fort had vanished.

"Maybe we really did dream he was alive," said Sally.

"Or maybe he's only alive at night," said Kevin. "He could have knocked down the fort before becoming a snowman again."

"Maybe," said Sally, but she looked doubtful.

That afternoon, the weather changed. "It's like spring out," said Papa as he went to the barn to milk the cows.

The snow on the trees started to drip. The sun continued to beat down on the field for the next few days, turning the snow to slush and leaving puddles on top of the pond.

By Christmas Eve, Mr. Snow's head had become no bigger than a melon. His body had shrunk to the size of a small child.

"Mr. Snow's disappearing!" said Sally. "We've got to do something!"

"Let's hope it snows tonight," said Kevin, "so we can build him up again. It almost always snows on Christmas Eve."

But at bedtime, the weather was still warm. Sally and Kevin sat on the floor of the living room, listening to Papa read *The Night Before Christmas*. Even though it was too warm for a fire, Mama had laid one in the fireplace. It was crackling as Papa read. When he finished, he closed the book and said, "Time for bed. Santa will only come if you're asleep."

"I want to leave Santa some milk and cookies," said Kevin.

He set them down carefully by the fireplace. Then he and Sally kissed Mama and Papa good night.

Before they went to bed, they knelt by Sally's window and looked out at the field.

"Poor Mr. Snow," said Sally. "He's dying. Isn't there anything we can do?"

"Not unless it snows," said Kevin sadly.

"I have an idea," said Sally.

She ran to the desk and got a marker and a piece of paper. Then she wrote a note:

Dear Santa,
Please take Mr. Snow up to the North Pole with you.

"Do you think Santa can read?" asked Kevin.

"Of course," said Sally. "He reads the letters from kids, doesn't he?"

Sally and Kevin left the note by Santa's snack. Then they went to bed.

The next morning, Sally woke up as the sun was rising. Instead of running downstairs to see all the presents, she looked out the window.

She saw a wet mark where Mr. Snow had been.

"Santa took him!" she gasped, racing into Kevin's room. "Santa took Mr. Snow!"

Kevin was already at his window. "Or else he just melted completely," he said. "It's still warm out, and the field is really muddy. He could have melted."

But when Sally and Kevin went to look for the note and milk and cookies, they were gone.

"You see?" Sally told Kevin. "Santa *did* find the note, and he *did* take Mr. Snow to the North Pole."

But Kevin wasn't so sure. He sat thinking as he ate his pancakes.

"Time for stockings," said Mama and Papa.

The stockings were hanging from the mantel. For a moment, Sally and Kevin forgot about Mr. Snow.

Kevin discovered chocolates and toy soldiers and marbles in his stocking. Sally found gumdrops, a beaded necklace, and some hair ribbons. But when she reached down to the toe, she felt a soft lump. Curled up like a kitten was her scarf, the one she'd wrapped around Mr. Snow's neck.

"Look!" she cried. "My scarf! Santa left it before rescuing Mr. Snow!"

"And here's Mr. Snow's mitten!" shouted Kevin. "Now we know Mr. Snow is all right."

And it was true. Mr. Snow had found
a wonderful new home.